WHEN AIDAN BECAME A BROTHER

By **Kyle Lukoff**   *Illustrated by* **Kaylani Juanita**

LEE & LOW BOOKS INC.
New York

When Aidan was born, everyone thought he was a girl. His parents gave him a pretty name. His room looked like a girl's room. And he wore clothes that other girls liked wearing.

But as Aidan got bigger, he hated the sound of his name.
He felt like his room belonged to someone else. And he
always ripped or stained his clothes accidentally-on-purpose.

Everyone thought he was just a different kind of girl.

Some girls had rooms
full of science experiments
and bug collections.

Lots of girls didn't wear dresses.

But Aidan didn't feel like any kind of girl.
He was really another kind of boy.

It was hard to tell his parents
what he knew about himself,
but it was even harder not to.

It took everyone some time to adjust, and
they learned a lot from other families with
transgender kids like him.

Aidan explored different ways of being a boy. He tried out
lots of names until one stuck. They changed his bedroom into
a place where he belonged. He also took much better care of
his new clothes.

Then one day, Mom and Dad had something to tell him.

"I'm going to have a baby!" Mom announced.

"A baby?" Aidan said. "Does that mean I get to be the big brother?"

"Of course," said Dad, ruffling his hair.

Aidan thought that being a big brother was an important job for a boy like him. He wanted to make sure this baby would feel understood right away.

The baby needed clothes, so Aidan and his mom
went shopping. There were so many choices!
Would the baby like seahorses or penguins better?

"Are you having a boy or a girl?" asked a lady.

Aidan didn't like it when people asked if *he* was a boy or a girl, and he hoped the baby couldn't hear yet. He was glad when Mom just smiled and said, "I'm having a baby."

The baby's room needed to be painted, so Aidan and his dad went to the hardware store. Dad chose a gallon of sky-blue paint, and Aidan added a puffy-cloud white.

"Are you excited for your new brother or sister?" asked the paint guy.

"I'm excited to be a big brother," Aidan said.

The paint guy looked confused. Aidan could tell that he wanted to ask a different question, and was glad to have his dad there.

The big rollers were fun to paint with. "This room feels just like being outside!" Aidan exclaimed. He had always felt trapped in his bedroom before they fixed it, but his new sibling wouldn't have to feel that way.

"You're right," said Dad. "Let's make some shapes in the clouds!"

Every baby needs a name. Aidan loved getting to choose his own, but he remembered that it had been hard for his parents to let go of the name they gave him. He looked for names that could fit this new person no matter who they grew up to be.

moss

leaf

cloud

rain

river

Babies need someone to read to them, so Aidan practiced

and practiced

and practiced.

Dad wanted to teach Aidan how to change diapers.

"Um, maybe later!" said Aidan. He decided that picking flowers for his mom was more important.

Two weeks before the baby's due date, Aidan started to worry. Maybe he should have picked different clothes. The blue walls might be too bright. He wished he could ask the baby which name they liked best.

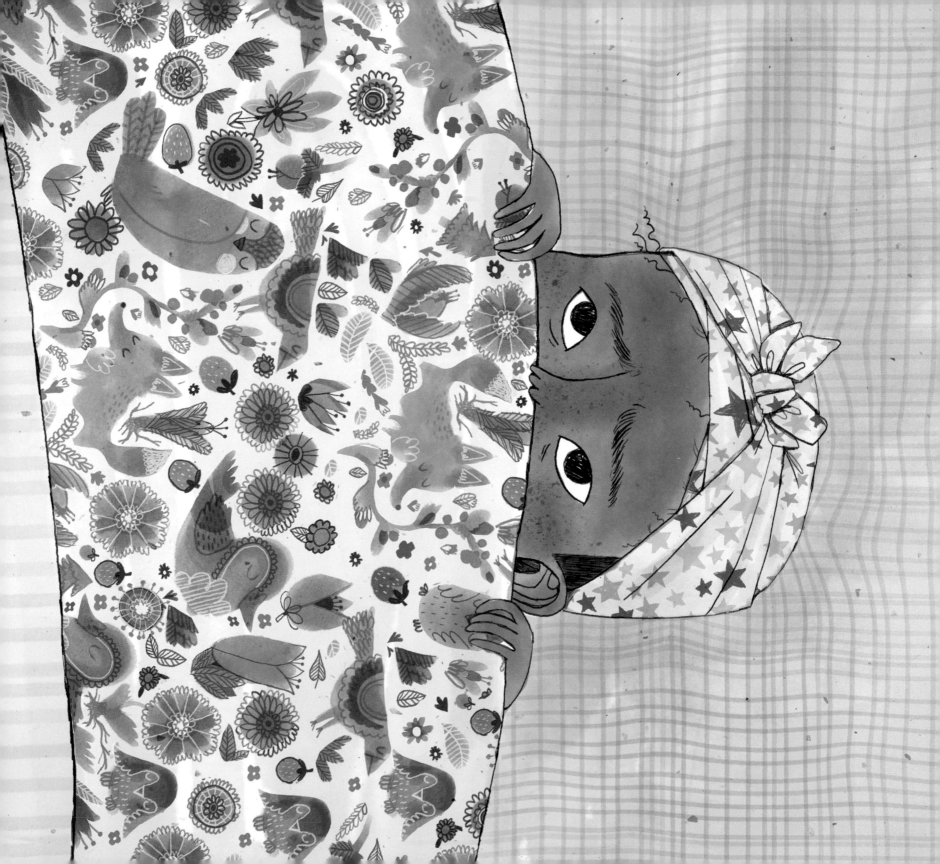

Mom came to tuck him in. "Are you feeling okay, sweetie?" she asked.

Aidan put his hands over where he thought the baby's ears would be. "Do you think the baby will be happy with everything?" he whispered. "I don't want them to feel like I did when I was little, but what if I get everything wrong? What if I don't know how to be a good big brother?"

Mom hugged him tight. "When you
were born, we didn't know you were
going to be our son. We made
some mistakes, but you
helped us fix them.

And you taught us how important
it is to love someone for
exactly who they are. This
baby is so lucky to have
you, and so are we."

The next morning, Aidan found the boxes of his old baby
pictures. He looked so different back then! It hadn't been easy,
but he liked the boy he was growing into.

Maybe everything wouldn't be perfect for this baby. Maybe he would have to fix mistakes he didn't even know he was making. And maybe that was okay.

Aidan knew how to love someone,
and that was the most important
part of being a brother.

AUTHOR'S NOTE

When I was born, everyone thought I was a girl. But my story is very different from Aidan's. I don't have a little sibling (but I do have a big brother!), I liked wearing dresses, and it took me much longer to discover that I was a boy.

Of course, some parts of my story are very much like Aidan's. That might be true for you too. If you're a kid who is transgender like Aidan (or transgender but not like Aidan), I'm hoping this story helps you understand what you're feeling, and helps you talk about it if you're ready.

You might also feel like Aidan in other ways. He knows what it's like to not quite belong, and you might feel that way sometimes too. People don't always see Aidan how he wants to be seen, and you might know what that feels like. Maybe you worry about making mistakes. Aidan is a transgender kid, but he's also just a kid. Like you.

Life for Aidan, and for all different kinds of kids, will be full of growth and change. I don't know what the future holds for him, but I hope he lives in a world that supports and believes in him. Thank you for helping to create that world.

To those who came before me, to those who came up with me,
and to those who will come after me—K.L.

To the older siblings who protect and cherish their younger siblings—K.J.

Text copyright © 2019 by Kyle Lukoff
Illustrations copyright © 2019 by Kaylani Juanita
All rights reserved. No part of this book may be reproduced, transmitted, or stored in an information retrieval system in any form or
by any means, electronic, mechanical, photocopying, recording, or otherwise, without written permission from the publisher.
LEE & LOW BOOKS INC., 95 Madison Avenue, New York, NY 10016 | leeandlow.com
Edited by Cheryl Klein | Book design by Abby Dening | Book production by The Kids at Our House
The text is set in Marco Regular. | The illustrations are rendered digitally.
Manufactured in Korea
Printed on paper from responsible sources
9 10 11 12 13 14 15
First Edition

Library of Congress Cataloging-in-Publication Data
Names: Lukoff, Kyle, author. | Juanita, Kaylani, illustrator. • Title: When Aidan became a brother / by Kyle Lukoff ;
illustrated by Kaylani Juanita. • Description: New York : Lee & Low Books Inc., [2019] | Summary: "Aidan,
a transgender boy, experiences complicated emotions as he and his parents prepare for the arrival of a
new baby"— Provided by publisher. • Identifiers: LCCN 2018050617 | ISBN 9781620148372 (hardback)
Subjects: | CYAC: Transgender people—Fiction. | Parent and child—Fiction. Brothers—Fiction.
Classification: LCC PZ7.1.L8456 Whe 2019 | DDC [E]—dc23 LC record available at
https://lccn.loc.gov/2018050617